Santa Monica

By

J. R. Laidley

Narrator

Love is a strange thing. It can engulf you and have you do things that you never thought you would do and it can also destroy you like it did, poor Romeo. Now who wants that? I sure didn't. I heard a song not too long ago where the lyrics said, love me before they all love me and then you won't love because they all love me. A few years ago I didn't understand what that meant. I would have never understood those lyrics or even know why love was so important until I took a random trip to London to celebrate New Year's Eve with a college friend of mine, and then it happen, the unexpected. You know I've never been one to believe in love at first sight. You hear about it happening to people in books, magazines, lame ass TV shows, and even movies but I never thought it could ever happen to me. It just wasn't something I ever considered in my universe. I mean I did believe in love but I have to admit sometimes I think, it might not be for everyone. Then she popped into my life so briefly and changed everything.

INT Airport Terminal

You enter through the security door and pass by TSA workers looking at the camera, directing you to walk to the right. You enter the terminal and there's people seating everywhere. All the seats are taken and people are even sitting on the floor. You see many frustrated faces. Then you zoom into a guy typing on his tablet with three seats open next to him for some strange reason.

Loud Speaker

Attention attention all passengers at Terminal D all flights will be delayed due to power outage. We are working on fixing the problem now. We will keep you posted via message board. Due to this inconvenience we are offering free food and drinks at the TGI Fridays in terminal D.

Passenger

What the fuck! I need to go home

Passenger 2

My sisters getting married, I can't miss it, Oh my god

Passenger 3

I don't want free food I want to go and see my family in Hawaii

Airport Security

Everyone just stay calm. They are working on the issue and will fix it as soon as possible

(Terminal D is packed with passengers. Babies are crying and people are frustrated. There are no seats for people to seat. Then four mid twenties women come walking into the terminal exhausted from their last night in town. The look around and see no seats. Then one of them taps the girl in the front and points to the only open seats next to another guy in his mid twenties. They girls rush over and throw themselves onto the seats.

(Victoria legs brushes against Rick)

Victoria

I'm so sorry

Rick

Don't be. Here you can take my seat. I'll stand

Martha

(Whispers to Victoria)

He's cute

Amanda

Wow a gentleman, chivalry isn't dead

Rick

Long night?

Victoria

If you only knew, we had one of those nights that you see in movies

Rick

A hangover night, I would love to hear about it

Victoria

No I can't, we promised not to talk about it ever

Rick

Well it's not like I'm going to tell anyone and by the looks of it we're going to be here for awhile

Jessica

Tell me about it

Martha

Wow you're really cute. How do you always find the cute ones
Vicky?

(Victoria blushes)

Vicky

Shut up Martha, he can hear you

Rick

So where are you lovely ladies heading too

Amanda

We're heading back to Australia, the cute girl next to you is
Victoria she's from London, Martha over there is from Toronto,
Jessica is from California, and Me, Amanda well I'm from New
York. We all went to college together and decided to move to
Australia after college. How about you cute boy?

Rick

(with a smirk on he's face)

My name is Rick and I'm from originally from Miami but I went
to school in Philadelphia but now I work in New York

Amanda

So I guess you're a rolling stone then

Rick

I wouldn't say that, I just can't stay stagnant in the same place
too long

Martha

So what brings you to London

Rick

I was visiting one of my best friends for New Years

Victoria

I'm a little hungry

Rick

You want to go grab something

Amanda

(smiles)

Yeah Victoria go, with Rick and get something to eat

Victoria

(Victoria looks over to Amanda and gives her a look. She then turns to Rick)

Let's go before it gets any weirder

(Rick nods and they walk off)

Amanda

She better not mess this one up

INT Restaurant

(Both Victoria and Rick are laughing)

Victoria

I'm serious stop laughing at me

Rick

You have to admit, you never wanted to go to Miami because you thought that you would get eaten by a gator

Victoria

Well when you put it like that it does sound crazy

Rick

Honestly we don't have gators in Miami just beautiful beaches and nice water. I would love to show you one day

Victoria

I bet you would

Rick

What's that suppose to mean

Victoria

You just want to see me in a bikini

Rick

I would be a liar if I said no, I mean come on your beautiful.
Who wouldn't want to see you in a bikini, even a gay guy would

Victoria

Oh stop

Rick

What it's the truth, don't like you don't know you're beautiful. I
bet all the guys try to talk to you when you walk into a room

Victoria

Honestly not really. I can't remember the last time I was able to
sit down with a guy and talk like I'm talking to you. Wow why
did I say that, oh you're good

Rick

I'm good

Victoria

Yeah you have me talking about me and I never talk about me
especially to strangers but for some reason you're different. I
bet you have all the girls in New York going crazy over you

Rick

No I work too hard to drive anyone crazy but myself

Victoria

So the cute guy isn't a ladies' man

Rick

So you think I'm cute

Victoria

We wouldn't be here talking if I didn't

Rick

True

(Victoria smiles at Rick)

Rick

This is just my luck.

Victoria

What? What's wrong?

Rick

I mean why now and why here of all the places

Victoria

Are you going to fill me in anytime soon?

Rick

What are we doing?

Victoria

I don't know, this can't work we live on the opposite sides of the
world

Rick

But it feels like it can and will

(IN runs Martha, Jessica, and Amanda)

Amanda

Vicky, we have to go now. They have a plane for us and we
have to go to leave now. Bye pretty boy

Victoria

(gets up grabs her purse and looks at Rick. Water comes to her
eyes)

We may never find out, bye Rick

(she turns around slowly and starts to walks out. Rick just sits
there and looks at her leaving. She turns around and runs back.
She kisses Rick passionately)

(Whispers in Rick's ear)

If it's meant to be we'll find each other again, I'll keep an eye
open for you

(She runs out after her girls)

INT Terminal Hallway

Amanda

Damn did you at least get his Facebook?

Victoria

No should I

Martha

No time for that now, we got to go. We have 5 minutes to get there

Jessica

I told you to use app bump to your phone but no, no one wants to listen to me

Victoria

Shut up Jessica it hurts enough let's get going

INT Restaurant

Rick

Waitress can I get a double

(He reaches into his pocket and takes out his phone. He pushes a few buttons and Skype turns on. His best friend in New York picks up)

Jason you were right it can happen

Jason

What the hell are you taking about man I'm playing xbox online right now killing it in call of duty

Rick

I found her man I found her

Jason

Ok this sounds serious let me get off damnit almost got the nuke

(Jason puts down the controller)

What's up

Rick

I met her

Jason

Who?

Rick

The girl of my dreams and I just let her leave

Jason

Wow this is serious especially coming from you. So who is she?

Rick

Victoria

Jason

Ok Victoria who? I want to check her out on Facebook to see the girl that got you

Rick

Oh shit I don't even know her full name

Jason

Are you kidding me. I'm going back to Call of Duty

Rick

No I'm serious man. Oh shit maybe I can catch her at her terminal

Jason

Yeah you go do that bye

(Rick leaves a fifty at the bar and runs out of the restaurant. He runs passes everyone, like a running back but as he gets to the gate he sees the plane lifting off. He put his head against the glass and closes his eye)

Airline Worker

Can I help you Sir was that your flight

Rick

(turns around and looks at the airline worker)

Yes, there was a passenger on that flight name Victoria. This is really important we just met here and it felt like I knew her for years but she had to run to catch this flight and I forget to get her last name. Can you help me please?

Airline Worker

Awww that's so cute but I can't help you. We're not allowed to give that information out to anyone

Rick

Please just this once, if you believe in love at first sight you
would

Airline Worker

Nope can't do it but if it's meant to be you'll see each other
again. Now I have to go bye

(She finishes typing on her screen and walks away)

Rick

(sits down)

V.O

All passengers on Flight 917 to New York's Kennedy Airport,
please be advise that we are about to begin the boarding
process

Rick

Damnit back to NYC

A panoramic view of a beach comes into focus and the camera
focuses on four guys walking the beach laughing and having fun.

Rick

That was three years ago. I never saw her again. I mean I tired,
to Google Victoria from London, living in Australia, I even
Facebook all Victoria's in Australia, that took really long. You
would be amazed of the amount of Victoria's living in Australia
on Facebook. It took me days but I was determine to find her.
After about a year and a half I gave up. I know a year and a half

kinda creepy but what would you do for love? Don't knock it
until your hit by cupid's arrow.

 After meeting Victoria, things weren't the same anymore. I
was tired of my life in New York. The SOHO/Upper East/West
lifestyle was great but I needed a change. Then I got a phone
call from my high school friend Kyle. I say high school because
we did start the same college but then he met an actress on
campus, started dating her and when she left for LA he went
too. They didn't stay together long but Kyle decided to stay, he
met some great connections while with her and since Kyle was
secretly paid, from his trust fund, he got into producing films.
So when he called telling me to move out to LA, he needed help
with his new company, I jumped on it ASAP. Now here we are
the four of us. Kyle is the one to the left of me, Ant is the one to
the right of me, he met Kyle out here in LA, he's a great guy but
can party really hard, like a Stifler from American Pie. The
original, not those other ones and to the left of Ant was my
other friend Rich, they guy I was kicking it with that New Years
in London. We met in college. This was the team. We helped
Kyle run his production company and let me tell you business
was great. I had the all access card out here. It helped me not
to think about her, I mean I was with all the hot chicks, driving
all the nice cars, and partying at all the hottest spots in LA.

EXT Beach Santa Monica

                              Kyle

Well gentlemen, I know you don't have shit like this back East or
                        in London right?

Rick

Yeah yeah we know Cali is the place. Remember I'm from Miami. A lot of beaches there

Anthony

You should have seen Rick last night in the club man

Rick to himself

Oh yeah I forgot to tell you I co-own nightclub with Kyle, The hottest nightclub in LA. All the stars party there and all the celebrities' events are there too.

Rick

I don't know what you are talking about

Anthony

I could have sworn that I saw him making out with that chick from that HBO show

Rich

WOW that's where I saw her before. Oh yeah, Kyle he was getting it in with her. They went up to the back room and I didn't see Rick the rest of the night

Rick

Ok fine it was her I couldn't turn her down. She's too hot and I can tell you she's a freak. She was popping pills the whole night

Kyle

Oh don't tell me you're into that shit too now

Rick

Hell no but I will fuck a chick who is

Guys

(All laugh and slap each other five.)

Hell yeah

Anthony

Damn right. Hey you want to hit that Jonah Hill house party this weekend

Rick

What else am I going to do

Rick to himself

And this was my new life. If I wasn't on some movie set making sure things go right, I was at the club doing the same, or out partying every day or night of the week with the boys. I mean we had money a lot of it and we knew everyone and they knew us. It was like the Goodfellas movie but without the mob and moving drugs shit. The only drugs we were into was marijuana. We smoked and I mean we smoked a lot of it. In the Entertainment business if you didn't do some type of drug you were an outsider and come on its Cali, everyone smokes. You couldn't find a corner where there wasn't a smoke shop. The funny thing about is I turned into exactly what I told Victoria what I wasn't, a ladies' man. I mean I was really good at it too. There's so many hot chicks in LA and they all want to be actress and shit and most will do anything to get a chance to live the life and I mean anything.

(Four beautiful ladies mid twenties walk pass the boys on the beach. The cute one winks at Rick)

Rick

Be right back

(Rick Walks away)

Rich

Do you ever stop?

Ant

No way not him

(Rick walks up to the group of ladies and starts to talk to them. He waves the boys to come over but they just stand and watch Rick. Rick finishes getting the cute girls number and walks back over to the guys)

Kyle

What they say

Rich

Oh now you want to know about them

Kyle

I have my reasons not to go over there

Rich

(shocked)

Really

Ant

So what did they say?

Rick

Well they are visiting from Cuba and wanted to know a good club to hit

Rich

Let me guess you invited them to the club

Rick

I'm sorry but don't you want hot chicks at the club

Kyle

He does have a point

Rick

I know I do. Actually they were really interested in Rich

Rich

They were?

Rick

Yeah, that's why I signaled you to come over

Rich

Oh

Rick

Oh you have one of the hottest Cuban girls I've seen wanting to talk to you and all you can say is oh

Rich

I mean they live in Cuba and I live in LA

Rick

Shut the fuck up. You got money you can fly out there or fly her out here come on

Rich

What

Rick

What man? Just make sure you're at the club tonight please

Rich

Fine

Rick

Jeez he makes it hard to hook him up with someone damn

Kyle

You know who Rich is interested in?

Ant

Oh yeah that fine ass chick, that works on the show

Rick

Yeah but he won't talk to her

Rich

Hey I will talk to her

Rick

Really I bet you a 10G's that the next time you see her you won't talk to her

Rich

Fuck you, I'm not a betting type of guy

Ant

Fuck that for a 10G's I'll talk to her fine ass

Rich

No the hell you won't

Ant

Well then you better or I will

Rich

Fine I will

Rick

You better because she'll be at the club tonight homie

Rich

What? No she's not

Ant

What you scared now, bitch?

Rich

What who's scared

Ant

You

Rich

Kiss my ass Ant plus she's not going to be there tonight

Rick

Want to bet

Rich

Yeah

Rick

(Takes out his phone and shows it to Rich)

Now what

Ant

What just happen?

Rich

You're an asshole

Rick

Damn I get called an asshole for helping

Kyle

What happen?

Rich

This asshole texted her and told her I would love to see her
tonight at the club

Ant

Ha I bet she said no right

Rich

No, hold up just because I'm not pimping the city like Rick
doesn't mean I can't close on someone

Ant

Really you can close?

Rich

I'll close on your mother asshole

Ant

I'll slap the shit out of you don't talk about my moms

Rich

Oh I'm sorry, so emotional about things

Ant

Fuck you! What did she say scared bitch

Rich

Why you so concern

Ant

Hey man I'm single at the moment

Rich

And

Ant

I'm just saying since you're too shy to talk I'll talk for you

Rich

Naw I'm cool, I got this one

Ant

Oh ok we'll see about that tonight

Rick

This is getting interesting

Ant

Is the bet still on

Rick

Yup

Ant

Well I want in. I'll put a 10G's on it too that he won't talk to her
and even if he does he won't close

Kyle

You guys are getting carried away

Ant

No we're not

Rich

You know what fuck it, I got a 10G's on it that I will

Kyle

Wow Rich you ok

Rich

I'm fine I just want to shut this asshole up once and for all

Ant

We'll see

Rich

Yeah we will brother

Rick

This is going to be a great night. Well if you don't talk to her at least you'll have the Cuban girl

Rich

I won't need her

Rick

Well then I will

Kyle

Looks like I have to be at the club tonight to see this. I mean 30G's on Rich closing

Rick

I can't wait

INT Production Studio Office

Rick

No, No fucking way am I going to let them in my club again. I don't care if he just got a 50 million dollar contract extension; his boys almost trashed my place last time. What, what do you have to offer me.

(Kyle walks into his office and sits down)

OK, OK, hold on just listen, for a second. I'll let them come back but they better behave themselves and guess what he has to buy 100 bottles upfront and I don't care if they don't drink it all. Plus during the press conference he has to mention the club and say it's the hottest in LA. Then we have a deal... Perfect see you guys tomorrow night.

(Rick puts the phone down)

What's up man?

Kyle

Chillin still recovering from last night

Rick

Yeah man it was crazy, the club was packed

Kyle

I know plus your boy sealed the deal last night

Rick

He sure did and I made a 5G's that night

Kyle

Like you need it

Rick

I don't but I had to have my boys back

Kyle

True. What you doing tonight?

(Phone rings, Rick signals Kyle to hold on and picks it up)

Rick

Hello, What? No fucking way. I don't care if she's the hottest movie star right now, no way am I giving her a free booth and free liquor. Is it Christmas?

(Kyle gets up and turns around to leave. Rick puts the call on mute)

Rick

Hold on bro, I'm free tonight, why what's up

Kyle

Can you meet me at the Restaurant at 8pm?

Rick

Yeah, what's up

Kyle

Nothing much

(Kyle reaches the door)

Rick

He bro are you going to give me a heads up on why we're meeting tonight?

Kyle

(Kyle turns back with a grin on his face)

Nope just relax

(Kyle turns around and walks out)

Rick

Ok fine listen. I'll let her do her thing at the club but that means any event that she's involved in must be at the club and she has to Tweet that we're the hottest club in LA that's why she came tonight... SO do we have a deal? ... Perfect see you tomorrow night.

Rick

(puts his phone down)

Yo Anthony what you doing?

Anthony

I got to get down to the studio and put out a small fire at the table reading. Why what's up?

Rick

I'll go with you

Anthony

Fine let's move out I got to get down there fast

Rick

Well let's take my car

Anthony

Whatever

Rick

Hey man don't get mad cuz you lost the bet last night

Ant

I ain't mad at that. Shit I'm happy for Rich plus it's only 10G's

Rick

My fault baller

(The guys start to walk towards the elevator. As soon as they get to the elevator the doors open)

Ant

So what's up

Rick

Kyle tell you about this dinner tonight

Ant

Yeah what you're worrying

Rick

What's it about? I mean he's been a little distance lately

Ant

Yeah he's got a lot on his mind lately

(As soon as the doors to the Elevator open and Rich is standing there)

Guys

Yo

Rich

Where y'all going

Anthony

Studio

Rich

Shit I'll come then

Anthony

Ok but that means we're not taking Rick's car

Rich

I'll drive. Don't really feel like being in the office too much today anyways

INT Car

Ant

Like you ever do shit when you're there anyways

Rich

Fuck you, you just mad because of last night

Anthony

Whatever Congrats Rich you finally talked to her, I mean damn secretly I was rotting for you. Figure that if I put a bet on it, you might be more motivated to go for it.

Rich

Whatever man you mad, don't worry you'll have your time to talk to a woman

Anthony

You forgot who you're talking too, I ran this city

Rich

Key word RAN

Ant

Whatever, I'm fine where I'm at right now

Rick

Seriously man he's kinda right you haven't been around a lot lately. What's up?

Rich

I've been helping Kyle out with a project

Rick

What project and why does it seem like I'm the only one who doesn't know about it?

Anthony

Just chill all will be revealed soon

Rick

What is this some secret society shit?

Rich

If it was some shit like that wouldn't you be the one initiating me? Remember you called me to come to Cali, not the other way around

Rick

I don't like not knowing what the fuck is going on. I mean come on help me out aren't we all brothers here

Ant

Just chill, Rick stop at In and Out or even Fat Burger, I need one

Rick

Aw hell naw don't eat that shit. You'll have a heart attack really soon if you keep eating that shit, Why don't we stop at that new organic burger joint

Ant

Hell naw they want like 15 beans for a burger and don't worry I work out a lot, so I can eat anything I want

Rick

Who told you that bullshit and you can afford a 15 dollar burger stop being cheap!

Anthony

It's the principal of the matter. Why only people with money can eat healthy? Huh it's a conspiracy. Plus I read it, in a Men's Magazine article that I could

Rich

Oh shit, so why don't you get into politics and change the standards. Hold up when did you start reading, Men's Magazine?

Anthony

Fuck you

Rick

The real question who were you trying to impress?

Anthony

Ok I may have been at the juice bar at the gym and there was this really cute chick there and my segway to talking her was the eating anything article that I just happen to open too.

Rick

Exactly what I thought it had to be some reason why you were reading. IF it isn't visual it gets no attention from Anthony and plus WTF you're at the juice bar at the gym that shit ain't cheap asshole

Anthony

Whatever dickhead and it worked and that's all I'm going to say. Now pull into that In and Out.

(Rich pulls over into the In and Out burger and Anthony hops out)

You guys want anything?

Rich and Rick

Nope

Anthony

Y'all don't know what you're missing

Rick

So you're really not going to tell me

Rich

Nope

Rick

Damn Judas I was the one that brought you in

Rich

Damn don't play that card, it's not the time for that

Rick

Fine

Anthony

(enters the truck)

Damn where are the cup holders in this expensive piece of shit

Rich

What the fuck it's a benz asshole

Anthony

Exactly, a German piece of shit, should have got the Audi one instead

Rich

You don't know shit about cars. Audi is German dick

Rick

Laughs

Anthony

No my friend I think that it's the other way around

Rich

Rick which cars better Benz or Audi

Anthony

You can't ask the guy who only wants to drive Italian

Rich

And why not

Anthony

His ass is bias

Rick

I'm not in this one. Shit I ain't talking to neither of you assholes right now

Anthony

Damn is it someone's time of the month

Rick

Fuck you, we're here anyways go take care of business

Anthony

Yes Boss is there anything else you want me to do while I'm out Sir

Rick

Yeah Go fuck yourself

Rich

Hey isn't that the girl you we're hitting last summer

Rick

Where

Rich

Over there by security crying

Rick

Oh shit, Heather

(Rick hops out of the truck and quickly goes over to Heather)

Rich

Typical ladies man

EXT outside Security

(Heather's crying and security lady next to her is standing with a clip board)

Security Lady

I'm sorry you are not on the list for the audition. I can't let you in

(Rick walks up)

Rick

Hey Jasmine how are you?

Security Lady (Jasmine)

Hey Rick

(with a grin on her face)

I'm fine thanks for letting me and girls in the club last week they had a ball

Rick

I saw that. Hey Heather how are you?

(Heather looks up and tries to wipe the tears from her eyes. While she lifts her eyes Rick has a tissue in his hand to give her)

Heather

Rick, what are you doing here?

Rick

I'm here with the boys just putting out a small fire on set why, what's the problem

Heather

(Still crying)

My agent told me to come here for an audition for that new HBO show and my name isn't on the list. Now I'm late for my audition and it was the perfect role for me

Rick

Ok here

(gives her a tissue)

Stop crying, I got it. Hey Jasmine

Jasmine

Just go Rick

Rick

Thank you Jasmine

(Rick and Heather go pass security and head towards the audition)

Heather

So looks like things are going well for the team

Rick

(smiles)

Can't complain but forget me what's new with you

Heather

You know I moved back to the City for a theater gig and now I'm back West.

Rick

Aw the City it's been awhile since I've been back.

Heather

Yeah I ran into Jason while I was out there

Rick

Damn seems like forever since I talked to him. How is Jason doing?

Heather

He's good got a promotion at his job but I think he's burning out from the Wall Street. You know since all this shit happen with the market. It amazes me how he kept his job and kept moving up

Rick

You know people who are just winners, no matter what they do they win, well that's Jason a natural born winner

Heather

Yeah I know

Rick

What's that suppose to mean

Heather

Oh nothing

Rick

Here we are, let me peek in and say Hi.

Heather

Should I stay here?

Rick

Naw come in with me

(Rick and Heather walk into the audition room. The casting director, Director, Executive Producer, and the lead actor is there wrapping up and getting ready to leave.)

INT Audition Room

Rick

What's up!

Executive Producer

Rick what the hell are you doing here?

Rick

Well I was at the security booth and I saw this lovely lady trying to get in for her audition and they wouldn't let her in

Larry (Lead Actor)

Such a good Samaritan

Rick

Whatever muthafucker. Guys this is Heather a great actresses but I'll let her to show you how good she is

Heather

Thank you Rick so much I owe you one

Rick

No worries, hit me up sometime

Heather

Ok

Rick

Jethro let me know when you're free we can hit the course
again

Jethro (Excutive Producer)

Will do Rick

Rick

bet

(Rick walks out of the audition room)

INT Hallway

(phone rings)

Rick

Yo

Anthony

Yo where you at we're ready to roll

Rick

Where you at

Anthony

My parking spot

Rick

On my way

EXT Parking Let

Rich

So Pimp, did you make out with her

Anthony

Who, what I mess

Rick

A lot, man it was just Heather

Anthony

Heather, the crazy bitch who almost drove her car into the house last summer

Rick

Yeah, that Heather. She's not that crazy someone gave her a pill and she never done pills before

Anthony

I think I hear that from every chick right Rich

Rich

Yeah they always say you know I don't do this

Rick

Ha, so true they all say that in the beginning then you get them out of the public eye and the real crazy comes out

Rich

True, let's get out of here I have a stop to make before we get
back to the office

Anthony

Yeah I'm getting hungry again

Rick

Damn doe boy what happen? what you got a girl now or are you
depress

Anthony

No I'm not depressed man can I live

Rick

Not the way you've been eating lately

Anthony

Whatever let's roll

(The guys drive off and leave the studio lot.)

INT Restaurant

The restaurant is packed. People are enjoying their meals and
taking in the ambiance of the luxury restaurant.

EXT outside Restaurant

It's packed outside. People are lined up trying to get in to see
the celebrities inside of the restaurant and camera flashes are
going off all the time. Rick drives up to valet with the top of his

car off. He hops out without opening the door and walks into the Restaurant quickly. He walks up to the front desk

Front Desk Clerk

Mr. Chambers, it's a pleasure seeing you again. Your party is in the back already. Let me have Jose walk you back there, Jose

Jose

Follow me Mr. Chambers

Rick

(Slides Jose a hundred dollar bill)

Come on Jose I told you to call me Rick

Jose

ok Rick but you know you don't have to pay me

Rick

No worries, hey man whenever you're looking for a change from the restaurant scene come to the club, I'm sure we can use you

Jose

Thank you Rick, here's your party

Kyle

Here he is my best man

Rick

What The Fuck is going on here

Kyle

Rick I want you to meet Christina, my fiancée

Rick

(coughs)

OH SHIT, HI Christina nice to meet you. Wow so this is what you've been up too

Kyle

Christina this is Rick the guy I've been telling you about.

Christina

(smiles)

Hi Rick, Kyle has told me so much about you

Rick

I hope only the good stuff

Christina

Well let's just say he tells me everything

Rick

Damn

Kyle

Nothing for you to worry about bro, I met Christian while I went out to the Swiss Alps, she was my ski instructor

Rick

Wow must have been one hell of lesson

Kyle

If you only knew, it was love at first sight. I told her that in order for us to make it official, she has to meet my boys. So Christina here are my boys, all of them

Rick

And who is this Anthony

Anthony

This is Rachael, the girl I told you about, you know the juice bar

Rick

Oh shit the one you lied to about reading that Men's Magazine

Anthony

(puts his head down)

Yes

Rachael

Don't worry, I knew what he was doing but I admired him even trying. Do you know how many men just stare at me at the gym, it's kinda creepy

Rick

Holdup it's you, the girl in that new superhero movie, oh shit I thought you rocked that role

Rachael

(smiles)

Thank you Rick

Rick

Hi Stephanie

Stephanie

Hi Rick what's new

Rick

Shit seems like everything is new now, damn I'm the only one here without a date

Rich

We wanted an intimate dinner

Rick

What I'm intimate, very intimate

Christina

I heard about how intimate you are Rick. From what I heard you have no problem in that area in your life. What's the term I'm looking for ah you're a playboy

Rick

Wow really that's what you'll think about me

Everyone

Yes

Rick

Damn that's fucked up

Anthony

Man it's the truth. Nothing wrong with being a playboy live it up man. You're young, work hard and play hard playboy

Rick

Screw you Ant

Kyle

Ok guys let's leave Rick alone he's happy living the life his living.

Rich

Kyle's right, tonight is all about Kyle and Christina

(Gets up with a glass of champagne)

Now let's toast the soon to be married happy couple

(Everyone gets up and toast to the couple)

Rick

So honestly Christina, what were your first thoughts when you met Kyle

Christina

You know when I got the assignment I was skeptical because the last few Americans I worked with were douches but when he walked into the room his energy overwhelmed me and then he said hi, I think I blanked out for about a minute and I knew he was different. Plus I love his smile, it just does thing to me

Anthony

Damn

Rachael

Shut up

Anthony

What no one has ever said to me that my smile does things to them

Rachael

(Kisses Anthony)

I love your smile baby

Kyle

This is what it's all about. I love all of you here. If we live forever I know we'll be happiest immortals ever

Rich

I have to admit when Rick called and said it was time to leave
London and move to LA, at first I thought he lost his mind but
now, it was the best thing ever for me.

(turns to Rick with his champagne glass)

Let's toast the best man, Rick, the glue that keeps this whole
thing together and the best friend a guy could ever have

(Everyone lifts their glasses)

Everyone

TO Rick!

Rick

Kyle, I've known you for decades and I can honestly say that you
are a great man. A man's man, I'm happy that you've found
Christina, and I hope you stay happy together for a thousand
years

Kyle

Thank you Brother, well listen guys a bunch of Christina friends
are coming to town next week to help her with the wedding, So
Rick, I need you to work with her maid of honor

Rick

Anything for you bro

(In walks Jose)

Jose

Mr. Chambers, you have a phone call

Rick

Who knows I'm here ok I'll be back

(Gets up and follows Jose to the back)

Kyle

(turns to Christina)

Are you happy?

Christina

Yes my love. You're friends are great. I can't wait for you to meet mine. hmm

Kyle

Is there something on your mind then

Christina

Just thinking my love, I think Rick will love Victoria

Kyle

I'm sure he will

(Rick walks back quickly)

Rick

I got to go guy, have an issue at the club that I have to take care of

Kyle

Really can't Jordan take care of it

Rick

Sorry bro, Jordan moved back to New York so I have to take care of this one but I'll get up with you guys tomorrow

Kyle

I'll walk with you out

Rick

Ok

(Kyle and Rick start to walk towards the door and Kyle places his arm around Rick)

Kyle

So tell me what you think Bro

Rick

You got a winner man. I'm proud of you and happy that you found one. Don't mess it up man

Kyle

Why do you think I've been away so much from the club and studio? I know if I'm around it I'll fall back into my old ways. Too many hot women around

Rick

Makes sense, well let me get back into the life so you can stay away

Kyle

(Stops walking and places both arms on Rick's shoulders)

I appreciate everything you do for me man, thank you

Rick

Man don't get all mushy on me, see you tomorrow

Valet

Your car Mr. Chambers

Rick

(Hops into his Lamborghini)

See you tomorrow bro

(Drives off)

INT Lamborghini

Rick

Damn, what have I turned into? Am I that guy now?

(Rick pushed a button on the dashboard and a voice starts to talk)

Voice

How can I help you?

Rick

Call Heather

Voice

Which Heather

Rick

Ah damnit, shit

Voice

Call damnit, no reference of that person

Rick

Smith, Call Heather Smith

Voice

Calling Heather Smith

Heather

Hello

Rick

Heather It's Rick

Heather

Hey Rick oh my God I have to Thank you so much I got a callback
for a series regular. I owe you so much

Rick

Oh no worries, I'm just happy I could help

Heather

Sounds like your driving, what's going on?

Rick

Yeah a situation at the club I have to go and handle, nothing
major. Hey what are you doing tomorrow want to grab lunch at
your favorite restaurant about 1

Heather

Oh you remembered, that's so sweet of you Rick. Yeah let's do
lunch and it's on me Mr. Bigshot, I owe you at least that

Rick

'ha, cool I'll see you tomorrow

Heather

Looking forward to it, see you then Rick

(line cuts off, Rick pulls up to the club and hops out)

Rick

Talk to me, what's the problem

Mark

Man, we're packed to capacity and that damn NBA asshole
wants us to let in twenty of his boys

Rick

(takes a look at the line outside, the paparazzi taking pictures,
and people trying to get his attention so they can get in and
shakes his head)

Fuck it let them in through the back and open up the top section
and let all these people in

Mark

Are you sure

(looks at Rick, Rick gives him a head nod and walks in. As Rick
walks in everyone notices him, the DJ gives him a shout out,
security clears a way for him to get to the VIP section. The club
is packed, people are drinking, dancing, and talking. Rick gets to
the VIP section a guard opens up the rope and Rick goes to each
booth and tells everyone hi. Rick walks up to the NBA player)

Player

Damn it's poppin tonight Rick

Rick

Yeah boy, you good!

Player

I'm great man we're in the playoffs. Here man, take a shot with
me

(The two takes a shot of tequila)

Rick

Alright let me make my rounds

(Rick heads over to the movie stars booth, it's packed with ten beautiful women)

Jennifer

HEY Rick, ladies this is Rick, he's the man and he runs this place

Rick

Oh stop, Hi Ladies are you having fun?

Jennifer

Hell yeah Rick, it's Tiffany's birthday

Rick

Hold up what it's your Birthday!

(Rick signals the bottle service girl and she comes over)

So Tiff you know what's next, right?

(Tiffany shrugs her shoulders)

Shots, Shots, Shots, bring over some Ciroc and shot glasses

Jennifer

I told ya Ricks the man

(Rick stays with the ladies and takes numerous shots with them. Rick sits by Tiffany)

Tiffany

So you run this place

Rick

Yeah and I'm a part owner with my boy

Tiffany

Wow

Rick

Want to see my office

Tiffany

Yeah

(Tiffany and Rick get up and start to walk away)

Jennifer

Don't do anything I wouldn't do girl

(Security sees Rick trying to move through the pack crowd and they escort them to his office)

INT Office

(Rick sits down by his desk and goes into his draw and takes out an already rolled joint and Tiffany sits on the Couch)

Tiffany

You're going to smoke in here

Rick

You'll soon learn that I do what I want

Tiffany

Oh ok Big Shot, you're da boss

Rick

Want some?

Tiffany

Hold up

(goes into her bag and takes out a pill and pops it in her mouth and then finishes her drink)

Ok Now I can

(They stay in the office and finishes the joint then Tiffany gets up and looks out of the window at everyone in the club)

Tiffany

Can they see me?

(Rick walks up behind Tiffany and whispers in her ear)

Rick

No

Tiffany

I've never done it in a club before

Rick

There's always a first time for everything

Tiffany

No I can't

Rick

Yes you can

(Rick spins Tiffany around and presses her body up against the window, he starts to kiss her , lifts up her dress, and then pulls back.)

Rick

(Whispers in her ear)

Tell me you want it

Tiffany

(whisper into Rick's ear)

You know I do, now give it to me daddy

(They kiss passionately, Tiffany starts to undo Rick's belt, while Rick's hand goes down Tiffany's chest, Rick picks her up and spins her around. They fall into the leather couch)

Knock, Knock

(Tiffany lying on top of Rick, quickly gets up and puts on her dress. Rick puts his pants on and starts to put his shirt back on)

Rick

What is it?

Mark

Man get out here we got a problem

Rick

Coming

(Turns to Tiffany)

You ok

Tiffany

Yes, go I'll be fine. I'm going back to the booth, we can finish
this later

Rick

Ok

(Rick walks out of the office and closes the door)

INT Hallway

Mark

Man we got a problem, that damn fool Chris is in here drunk as
shit causing problems

Rick

Man you came to me with this bullshit

Mark

You know, you're the only one he listens too drunk

Rick

Fine let's go

(They walk down the stairs and head towards Chris)

EXT Street in front of cab

Rick

Here's a hundred bucks make sure he gets home safely

Cab Driver

For a hundred, you want me to tuck him in too

Mark

Don't get smart

Cab Driver

Sorry, I'll make sure he gets home. I mean it's only five block away, what I mean is Thank you

(Jennifer and the girls walk out just as the cab drives away. Rick turns to see them)

Rick

Leaving already

Jennifer

Nope, just taking the party to my place, you know where it is right?

Rick

Of course I do

Jennifer

Well don't be late and tell your friend to come too. We can all have some fun

(Rick smiles at the comment. Jennifer's limo pulls up and the girls get in)

Hurry up

Rick

We're on our way right now. Jim get my car now

Jim

Yes Sir

Mark

Damn, it never ends with you huh

(Jim pulls up in Rick's car)

Rick

(hops in)

Welcome to the life. You coming?

Mark

(looks up to the sky)

Hell yeah

(jumps in the passenger side and they pull off)

INT Morning Jennifer's room

Rick is in bed with Jennifer and Tiffany. Rick phones goes off ten times. Rick wakes up suddenly and looks to see it's 1pm

Rick

Oh shit oh shit damnit

(reaches for his phone and looks at it. 4 Missed phone calls from Heather. He presses redial)

Heather

Hello

Rick

Heather I'm so sorry, I got caught up in an important meeting about a movie.

Heather

So I guess you're not coming

Rick

I'm on my way now, I'll be there in thirty minutes. Is that ok?

Heather

It's ok Rick, see you in thirty

(Rick shakes his head and looks around the room for his clothes. He sees his pants and shirt. He softly gets off the bed and puts his clothes on.)

Rick

Mark you here, Mark you here?

(Rick walks out of Jennifer's room and walks down the hallway to the other master bedroom. He opens the door to see Mark and three other girls sleeping on the bed. He closes the door, walk down the steps, and heads out of the front door into his car. He opens the trunk and opens a briefcase with mouthwash, floss and a clean t-shirt. He quickly puts on the shirt, flosses, and uses the mouthwash. He hops into the driver seat and takes off)

INT Restaurant

(Rick rushes into the restaurant and sees Heather sitting at a corner table. He walks over and sits across from her)

Rick

I'm so sorry about this, I never thought it was going to last that long

Heather

No I know you're a busy guy it's cool. Hey I owe you. HBO just called and they are making me a series regular on the show

Rick

Wow congrats, so you really did rock it

Heather

Yeah but are you ok? You look a mess Rick, what kind of meeting was it

Rick

Do I? I'll be back, have to use the bathroom

(Rick gets up and leaves his phone on the table. Heather continues to eat and look around at everyone at the restaurant. Then Rick phone goes off, it's a text message. Even though his phone's lock you can see this message. It's from Jennifer, asking where he rush off too, they looking forward to round three with him. Rick comes back but right before Heather puts the phone back down)

Sorry about that needed to check myself

Heather

Your phone was buzzing

Rick

(looks down at his phone and sees the message from Jennifer and shows no reaction)

Oh ok

Heather

So you had a meeting huh? For a movie? What a porn movie?

Rick

You looked at my phone

Heather

You know what Rick, I came here for two things, to say sorry for last summer. I mean damn, I use to really like you but you've changed. You're MR. Hollywood now. It's too bad cause you were such a great guy. I don't know when you went bad but you did real bad.

Rick

Wow, What was the other thing

Heather

I wanted to talk to you was to tell you that me and your friend, Jason are dating and talking about getting married. We hoped that it won't be a problem because you two are friends but your Mr. Hollywood now, a heartless, superficial bastard now so why would it matter to you anyways

(Heather gets up)

Goodbye Rick, I wish you the best with your new life as an asshole

(Heather Leaves, Rick sits there with a blank look on his face. His phone goes off. It's another message from Jennifer asking him to come over. He signals the waitress for the check)

INT Office

Rich

(walks by Rick's office and sees Rick looking terrible)

Damn man, I spoke to Mark said you guys had a hella of night and day

Rick

Yo am I Mr. Hollywood? Have I changed?

Rich

(Walks in and takes a seat)

(yells)

Anthony, Kyle get in here now

Rick

Don't call them please

Rich

No you need the crew now.

(Kyle and Anthony walks in)

Anthony

What the fuck happen to you

Rich

Not the time take a seat guys

Kyle

What's up

Rich

Go ahead

Rick

Have I passed the point of no return, like there's no way for me to find what you guys found?

Kyle

Oh that's what this is about. What is my marriage getting to you?

Rick

Honestly, yes. When I came out here, you guys were living the life but at some point, you'll stopped and I kept going

Anthony

You're young bro, I might be just a little older than you but I've been out here doing the Hollywood life since I was a kid remember. I know sometimes I may wild out but no way near as I did before I met Kyle and you guys. Enjoy your youth, you're still new to this brave new world and you're not like your boy over here Rich. He never wanted anything to do with the life. Honestly, he's just here to help the business and make a lot of money doing it. Kyle over here found someone that makes him happy and helps him cope with the craziness of the business that we're in. Trust me you will find someone too.

Don't let it get to you. Live your life to the fullest my friend and when that someone comes around, you'll know.

Rich

Damn Ant, you left me with nothing to say. Shit you're smarter than you look

Anthony

Fuck you

Rich

Naw I'm serious man all the fun and games aside Rick, Ant's right. Don't get discourage, and don't go out there looking for it either let it find you

Kyle

He's right, Christina found me, I didn't go looking for it

Anthony

So cheer up! Go to the club tomorrow and pop bottles and take a fine ass chick home with you

Kyle

Plus Christina's girlfriends are coming here from all over the world, to help her with the wedding. You never know, the one might be one of her girls. Christina thinks you might like her friend Victoria

Anthony

Just don't give up hope playboy

Rick

I won't guys thanks I needed that pep talk

(The guys walk out of the office and Rick leans back into his chair)

(Rick to himself)

I always looked at Anthony as the wild guy, just out right fucking crazy but it all made sense why he acted the way he did. He grew up in this mad house called LA. He's been through the ups and downs of the crazy place and I believe he's seen it all but he hit the nail on the head, they all did. You should never chase after it. I did meet the one but, I lost her and never saw her again. Deep down I always knew she was the one but maybe she just wasn't the one right then. I still think about her from time to time. What can I say sometimes, someone comes into your life and makes that type of impression that you'll never forget and that's what she did to me.

Anthony

Yo grab your coat we're rolling to Rachael movie premiere and we're doing the after party at the club

Rick

Wait what no one didn't tell me this

Anthony

Last minute, let's roll

(Rick get up and walks out of his office)

INT Hallway

The four guys start to walk down the hallway. Anthony taps
Rick on his shoulder.

Rick

What's up

Anthony

I need your help. I really like Rachael, but I have to get her
friends to like me

Rick

Ok so

Anthony

The only problem is that I think I slept with one or two of them
back in the day

Rick

Here we go

Anthony

No it's not like that. I really like this one. That's why I need
your help tonight at the club Rick

(Rick to himself)

Wow this is serious he called me Rick

Rick

Ok Ant, tell me what you need

Anthony

I need you on your A game. I need the playboy, the baller, the shot caller, the ladies man, I need you to get her girls to love me. Can you do that for me?

Rick

(puts his hand out to Anthony and Anthony shakes it and they hug)

For you ok. Let's make this a night they'll never forget

(The guys get into the limo outside)

Rick

That night our publicist and the promotion team had the club packed with celebrities and I mean all of them it seem from movies, to TV, to sports, and even those so call reality TV stars. They were all there and we partied all night long. I really wasn't in the feeling in the mood to be that guy again but for Anthony I turned it all the way up. I had the DJ shouting out Anthony and Rachael, had bottles flowing to our booth nonstop, and I even open up the back room and had the afterhours running until 5am. I mean, they were hammered. By the end of the night, we did it.

INT Hallway club

(The whole group is walking out of the club.)

Anthony

Thank you Bro!

Rachael

(drunk)

Yeah thank you Rick, this was the best night I've had in awhile. Right ladies?

Ladies

(drunk)

Hell yeah are we doing it again tonight?

(Anthony and Rick look at each other and smile)

Rick

Sure, just make sure you'll get home safely tonight

Rachael

Aren't you guys coming with us

(Rick to himself)

I didn't even have to look Anthony's way. I told him I got him so I do. International playboy mode on

Rick

Of course we all can hop into the limo. There's enough room
for everybody

(They all get into the limo, Rick the last one looks up into the sky
first for a moment, shakes his head, then gets into the limo, and
the driver closes the door. The limo drives off, while the sun
starts to creep into the sky)

INT Rachael House Bedroom

(Rick wakes up sleeping next to three of Rachael friends. There
are pills on the floor and a half smoked joint on the night stand.
He quietly gets off the bed and puts his clothes on, grabs the
joint on the nightstand and walks out of the house. The limo is
gone. He takes out his cell phone and calls Richard.)

Rich

Yo, what time did you leave the club last night?

Rick

I don't know, Where are you

Rich

On my way to the office. Why

Rick

I'm up in the hills can you come get me

Rich

Yeah sure text me the address

(Rick text the address to Rich and puts the phone into his pocket and sits down on the steps outside of the house. He takes out the joint and smokes it waiting for Rich to come)

(Rick to Himself)

As I sit here reflecting on my life, smoking this joint, I ask, is my life really that bad? I mean, I'm living the dream, I'm sleeping with the hottest chicks in LA and in the entertainment business, making a lot of money and I mean a lot, I eat the finest food, and party at all the exclusive spots. I mean, when someone asked me what I do, I honestly tell them, I do what I want. I'm free and I have a crew that I can truly trust and that's worth more than anything in the world. I could retire right now and still live the life forever with the money I've made since I moved to California. Then why am I sitting here smoking this joint and wanting more. 9 out of 10 people in the world will only see this life on TV and I'm living it, the good life. So you know what I'm going back to living the good life, fast cars, great friends, good weed, and sleeping with the hottest woman around. Why not, I'll do it for the ones who can't.

(Rich pulls up and Rick sees him, gets up front the steps, throws the joint away, and hops into the car)

INT Car

Rich

You ok, you sounded like something was wrong, on the phone

Rick

Nope, nothing at all, it's all good my friend.

Rich

Oh I thought you were still thinking about that Mr. Hollywood
comment

Rick

I won't lie to you at first it bother me but now fuck it. I'm still
young and they say you only live once unless you're one of
those lame ass Vampires or like Superman and shit. So I'm
going to enjoy this good life we have out here man

Rich

YOLO

Rick

YOLO

(rick to Himself)

So after Rich drop me off at my car I decided to get back into my
zone and go hard and I mean GO HARD. I mean I have the all
access card to the City of Angels and it's time to use it. So I
decided to get back into the gym because like Kanye said got to
have it tight. I forgot how much fun I have at the gym too. You
see those two hot chicks over there, I slept with the two of
them, one crazy night in Baja, the twins on the treadmill, yeah
them too, ha ski trip. Didn't do a lot of skiing come to think of it
I don't remember even seeing the slopes but I did see a lot of
slopes. Oh yeah, I probably slept with about 60% of the woman
in here and now I'm here to let them know I'm back and it's on.
So while leaving, I give them a wave and trust me they will be at
the club tonight. One thing I've learned about LA girls is that

they love the life and most will do anything to experience it. So here we go!

EXT Night Club

(Rick pulls up and his phone rings it's Anthony)

Rick

Hello

Anthony

I fucked up Rick I fucked up

Rick

What, what are you talking about bro

Anthony

I love her bro and now she won't talk to me at all bro

Rick

What happen talk to me

Anthony

She found out she knows

Rick

Knows what

Anthony

About me and her best friends

Rick

Shit her friends

Anthony

I don't want to be without her

Rick

Man you just met her like a month ago is it really that serious

Ant

Yeah man and I fucked it all up

Rick

Ok we can fix it bro trust me we can

Anthony

No we can't it's over, it can't be fix, I'm done

Rick

Ok calm down buddy and tell me where you are right now

Anthony

I'm at our celebration spot, I figure it would be the best place
for it

Rick

For WHAT

Ant

For me

Rick

Ant, do me a favor and promise me you won't do anything crazy until I get there

Anthony

Ok, Fine

Rick

(conference calls Kyle and Rich)

Kyle and Rich

Yo

Rick

We got a problem

Rich

Man what did you do now?

Rick

(pauses, a look of confusion, than anger, then back to calm)

Ok I'm not going to comment on that but you guys need to meet me at the celebration spot

Kyle

Why what's up

Rick

Nothing good, it's Anthony and I don't think he's in the right
sense of mind

Kyle

I'm in my car now

Rich

On my way

Rick

Jose where's my car?

Jose

Johnny put it in the lot for you

Rick

I need it tell him to bring it back, I have an emergency.

Jose

Ok

Rick

Listen Jose make sure nothing goes wrong tonight

(Car pulls up and Rick hops in)

Call me on my phone if anything goes wrong

Jose

Ok Rick

(Rick pulls off)

EXT Hollywood Sign

(Rich pulls up first and runs to where Anthony should be, then
Kyle pulls up to see Rich running, he follows, then Rick sees Kyle
and follows)

Rich

Anthony Ant

Kyle

Ant man where are you bro

Rick

Please no Please no ANTHONY, SHIT

Rich

Anthony

Kyle

Where the fuck is he

Rick

(nervously)

I don't know I hope he did

Rich

Did what

Kyle

Let's not think about that let's find him

(They continue to walk and as soon as they go pass a tree, they see Anthony lying on the ground looking up at the sky. They guys run toward him)

Rick

Anthony Anthony

Kyle

Ant you ok

(he just lays there and says nothing for a moment)

Kyle

See anything interesting up there Bro

Anthony

You know the sky is quite beautiful at night. I wonder what's up there. Do you think we are alone in this vast universe?

Rich

Naw Bro we're probably not alone out here

Rick

Who knows there might be aliens like Aquaman out there Bro

(The guys lay down beside Anthony and look up at the sky together)

Anthony

You think I could find someone out in space for me, guys

Rich

I mean anything is possible, Bro why

Ant

Cuz I've ruined all my chances here on Earth

Rick

You ok Bro

Ant

...

Kyle

You ready to talk Bro?

Anthony

I never knew my playboy lifestyle would ever catch up to me. I mean come on, it's LA everyone sleeps with everyone. I mean damn even married couples do it, it's just the business that we're in. But this time it came back and crushed me. My heart is broken in so many pieces right now, I don't even want to continue living

Rick

Damn Bro, it's not that bad

Anthony

Someone once told me, You haven't really lived until you've fallen in Love. Because until you do, you can't accurately measure life. I didn't know what he meant until now. We only knew each other briefly but in that brief moment together I knew it was her. Now I'm lost. My life has no meaning without her

Rick

You're not lost Brother, we won't allow it at all. You have a dream team here. If you want her back, then all you have to say is that.

Ant

I do

Rick

Ok then. So what if you fucked this whole town. That was before you too even met. I'm sure she might have slept with someone you know too right?

Anthony

(Hesitate)

Probably but that's not going to help me now, just makes me feel worse than I do now

Rick

All I'm saying is that don't give up on hope, Anthony. If she's
the one, you'll try anything to get her back Right?

Ant

I guess

Rich

You guess man, you better know cuz I'm not here laying on this
fucking ground for a guess

Ant

Well

Kyle

Well what? Are you ready to fight for her?

Rick

So are you ready to try anything?

Ant

Sure

Rick

Fuck that, are you ready to try anything?

Anthony

Yes I am

Rick

Good let me work my magic

Rich

Are we done star gazing, cause my back is killing me

Rick

Sorry old man, I forgot we got MR. AARP over here

Rich

Fuck you I hurt myself playing ball this week

Rick

You playing ball with who

Rich

Just some people

Kyle

Naw man you're not getting away with that shit. Who got your ass to play ball

Rich

Ok fine it was Stephanie and her co workers.

Rick

Ha I knew it

Rich

She asked me to do her a favor, WHAT

Anthony

Oh nothing, the things we're willing to do for love right, Rick

Rick

Absolutely, well gentlemen, I must head back to the club

Kyle

(looks at Anthony)

Trust him

Anthony

I do

(Anthony, Rick and Kyle get up)

Anthony

Old man you need help getting up

Rich

OLD MAN! You know what next time I get a phone call about you might be in some trouble, you know what I'm going to say

(Anthony helps Rich get up)

I'm going to keep my old ass is in bed, I'll see his ass tomorrow

(Guys laugh)

Anthony

Damn it's like that

Rich

Yeah that's how you made it, calling my ass old, dickhead

Anthony

I should just push your old ass back down

Rich

Try it

Rick

Awe like a happy married couple

Rich

Don't you have some where to go asshole. Talking about doing whatever it takes for love huh. What ever happen to Australia Rick?

Rick

(puts his head down and shakes it)

Damn that's a low one

Anthony

Hold up what I miss

Rich

Nothing just me firing a shot.

Kyle

Ok guys leave Rick alone he's had a hard week and I'm going to need him at 100% nest week

Rich

Fine but just don't call me old

Anthony

Old

Kyle

Ant

Anthony

Ok ok fine, I would call his old ass old

Rich

(picks up a small rock and throws it at Anthony)

Anthony

See if your ass could see you would have hit me

(Rick throws another rock and this time it hits)

Anthony

Bitch

Rich

Yeah who's the bitch now? Huh, how you feel now?

Anthony

I'ma fuck you up that's how I feel

Rich

Bring it Bitch, don't let me call Rachael and tell her you're trying to put my ass in the hospital. You'll never get her back

Rick

Damn Rich, you're on some George Bush, shit. I don't care if you not attacking. I am attacking

Kyle

Ok guys I'm heading back to my fiancée. I'll probably see you guys later on in the office

Rick

Right behind you

(Kyle and Rich turn around and start to walk away)

Rich

Hold up, you're not leaving me here

(Rich and Anthony catches up to Kyle and Rick. They leave the Hollywood sign, go to their cars and drive off)

INT Car

(Rick's driving through Hollywood)

(Rick to Himself)

Damn do I really want to be so emotionally attached to someone that I would consider to end my life if we are no longer together? I mean we all read the Romeo and Juliet story in school and if you were like me, you said you must be out of your fucking mind. Not me. I mean there are more women than men in this world. So what if that one leaves, there will be another one right? Shit I hate Richard, as soon as I finally stop thinking about Vicky, he brings her up. The moment where I'm at that point where I throw in the cards on Love and the one.

See the question is this, Do I want what Kyle and Anthony have? Do I want that type of relationship where you would die for the other person? Where you would give up your freedom and this lovely life to share a different type of lifestyle with someone else? Well we'll just have to see because right now that one isn't in my life but would I even let her in if she was, damn what am I thinking? Time to get back to the real world

EXT Club

(Pulls up to the Club)

Club Girl

Hi Rick

Rick

(Waves and smiles to the girls outside of the club. Walks up to Jose)

Tell me some great news Jose

Jose

PACKED and I mean PACKED. All the booths rented out and we
have four booths that bought 10 bottles a piece. Plus this line
outside is getting bigger and bigger

Rick

How the hell did this happen

Jose

My cousins work at most of the major tourist hotels in town and
I told them what you did for me today and they said they are
going to tell everyone to come here.

Rick

(hugs Jose)

Damn playboy you're a primetime player. You never know what
someone is going to do with an opportunity until you give it to
them. Great Job my friend

Jose

My cousin knows the promoter at the XO club Monday nights

Rick

Yeah

Jose

Yeah, he's not happy with the new owners and looking to leave

Rick

Really

Jose

I could introduce you guys and he could bring that crowd here

Rick

Damn the XO on Mondays is always packed. Yeah tell him that I want to meet

Jose

Cool

Rick

Alright let me hit the office. You got it down here

Jose

Yup

(Rick shakes Jose hand and enters the club, Jose looks up to the sky and smiles)

INT Rick's Condo Bedroom

(Alarm going off. Rick pulls the cover off of him and presses the off button)

(Rick to Himself)

So I promised Ant, that I would take care of his relationship problem like a God Damn Doctor Phil. So that's what I'm going to do. How you may ask, well let me show you. Remember, she's an actress and I found out from her publicist who you see next to me in bed that, she has some reshoots for her new movie today at the studio. So my plan is to go down to the studio and have a conversation with her but after another round under the sheets with this beautiful publicist.

Publicist

You Ready baby

Rick

Absolutely

(Rick pulls the covers back over him and starts to kiss her under the sheets. Then his phone rings. He continues to kiss her even more passionately. As they kiss her hands move up and down his back with her placing her nails into his back ever so softly. The phone continues to ring

Publicist

(Whispers into his ear)

Forget it don't stop please

(Rick continues to ignore the ringing, until both his condo and his cell phone starts to go off)

Rick

I'm sorry but this might be an emergency

(Rick Stops and reaches for his phone)

Rick

Hello

Anthony

(hesitantly)

Any progress

Rick

Awe damn man it's you let me give you a call back later on

Anthony

Ok

Rick

I'm on it buddy trust me I'm on it

Anthony

I know talk to you later than

(Rick puts the phone down)

Publicist

Who was that?

Rick

A friend in need of my help

Publicist

Damn good looking, loyal friend, and great in bed, how are you single?

Rick

Ha, funny question. So what time did you say Rachael was going to be at the studio?

Publicist

In an hour, you know she's dating your friend right or was?

Rick

I'm not trying to date her, we don't do that to each other. Plus she broke up with him

Publicist

Yeah she did because he slept with her friends

Rick

That was before they even knew each other

Publicist

Shame too because she really loves him. She's heart broken right now

Rick

Good to know.

(gets up from the bed and starts to put his clothes on)

Well listen you're more than welcome to stay here but I have to
get out of here to catch up with her

Publicist

That's fine I have a lunch date with my husband anyways

Rick

Husband?

Publicist

Yeah I'm married, hey as long as you keep it on the low it
doesn't matter. You should remember that for the future

Rick

Got it well bye sweetheart and thanks for the info

(Rick finishes up putting his clothes on and leaves)

EXT Studio Set of Movie

Director

Ok Rachael we need to do another take

Rachael

Another one, I need five

Director

Ok Five

(Rachael walks off escorted by an AD to her trailer, she's on the
Phone with her agent)

Rachael

No I can do it, I'm just messed up right now. I need five minutes
then I'll be ok

(Rachael enters her Trailer and the AD walks away)

Rachael

(As she enters the trailer she turns her head to see Rick sitting
on the couch)

What the fuck are you doing in here? How did you get in here?

Rick

Don't ask don't tell

Rachael

What do you want Rick?

Rick

I just want to talk to you

Rachael

About what your, boy?

Rick

Yes

Rachael

I don't want to talk about him, it hurts too much. I can't believe
it and my so call girls didn't even tell me at first

Rick

Quick question, why the fuck does it matter who someone slept with before you

Rachael

It just does

Rick

Now that's not an answer and you know it. Tell me you don't still love him

Rachael

I do I do still love him which is why it hurts so much

Rick

And he loves you the same way you love him maybe even more

(Takes a seat next to Rachael)

Anthony is a great man. He's loyal, a gentleman, and a great friend

Rachael

I know he is Rick, those are some of the things I love about him

Rick

So how much do you love him Rachael

Rachael

You ever look at someone and think damn I would do anything for this person. Then they look at you and tell you don't ever change and they beg you not too and you ask them why and then they tell you because you're perfect just as you are

Rick

Wow, no I haven't

Rachael

Well that's how much I love him. I would change my whole lifestyle for him but he's one of the first men to come into my life and say you're perfect just as you are. That made me feel something on the inside that I've never felt before. I can't believe I'm telling you this, who are you? I've never admitted this to anyone not even my friends

Rick

I grew up in a house with three women, so I naturally have the ability to just talk to them

Rachael

Wow, they set you up to be a pimp, no wonder why everyone calls you that. It's really not your fault. I see why women love you so much. You look great and know how to talk to us. Damn

Rick

Trust me I know it's a gift and a curse but tell me more about Anthony

Rachael

What more can I say, that I would have his baby if he asked cause I would. Oh my God, I can't believe I said that. I can't believe I'm telling you all this, please don't tell him I said this please Rick promise me

Rick

(smiles)

Only if you promise me that you will give him another chance

Rachael

Damnit

(looks up at Rick and smiles)

For some strange reason, I trust you. With friends like you around him, I know he won't do anything to ever hurt me. So I promise

Rick

(smile and puts out his pinky)

Pinky swear

Rachael

(wraps her pinky around Rick's)

I swear… You know you're really a great guy Rick. You're just like my Anthony. When you find the right one, you'll stop

(Rick just looks at her and nods. Rachael gets up and starts to walk out of her trailer, then turns back with a smile on her face)

Thank you Rick, Thank you for allowing me to open up to you and not judging me. I really needed that, I'm going to call him as soon as I get a break today from shooting but I really want to call him right now damn. I feel so much better now. He's a blessed man to have you, Rick

(Rachael walks out of the trailer and Rick takes a long breathe, looks up, and then gets up and walks out)

EXT Trailer

Executive Producer

(leaned up against the trailer)

When you called and said that you can fix the problem I'm going to have today. I just trusted you. You're a game changer man. I hope your happy where you are and they appreciate what you do for them because if you're not please let me know. I'll have a position waiting for you

(Rick and the EP shakes hand, Then EP walks away)

Rick

Another hard day on the job, Well time to hit up the Coffee Bean

(Phone Rings)

Hello

Kyle

Meet me at the office we need to talk

                    Rick

                     Ok

(Hangs up the phone)

          Damn it never seems to end for the kid

INT Production Studio Office

                    Kyle

(On the Phone)

   Ok sweetheart let me handle it. Rick walking into the office
          right now. Let me talk to him about it

(Rick walks in)

           Let me call you back baby

(Hangs up the phone)

                    Rick

                 What's up

                    Kyle

          I need you to do me a favor

                    Rick

                     Ok

                    Kyle

See the wedding dress designer that Christina loves is going to be in San Diego and he only has a small window to meet with her

                         Rick

                          Ok

                         Kyle

The problem is that her friends are flying in tomorrow but we have to be in San Diego when their flights arrives

                         Rick

              So what you want me to pick them up

                         Kyle

Yes and no, I want you to pick them up but I want you to take them out and show them a good time. I promise you we'll be quick. As soon as we finish I'll hop on the helicopter and get back here to take over

                         Rick

(Takes a breathe)

                How many of them are there?

                         Kyle

Well that's the issue, there's eight of them and they don't get in
                    at the same time

                         Rick

  Oh shit so multiple trips to Santa Monica. What The Fuck Kyle

Kyle

Please for me

Rick

What about Anthony or Rich

Kyle

Well Anthony, handling his relationship issues and Rich is not that good of a people person. I need you

Rick

(looks down and shakes his head then looks up at Kyle)

Fine but you owe me for this one

Kyle

Deal

INT Limo outside of Airport

Driver

(wind down the privacy window)

Sir, looks like the first three girls flight is delayed thirty minutes. Do you want to stay?

Rick

Yeah what else am I going to do. Let's just stay I'm going to fix me a drink

(Phone Rings)

Yo

Kyle

How's it going?

Rick

Shit flights delayed thirty minutes so I'm here just camping out drinking and about to smoke this joint

Kyle

Everything ok Buddy

Rick

I'm good fam, just tired. I think I need a vacation

Kyle

Once we're done with everything, take a break. The team can handle it for a bit while you rejuvenate yourself

Rick

Yeah, I'll take you up on that one

(Rick smokes his joint, plays on his Surface, and starts to pass out)

Driver

Sir we have another update looks like both flights are arriving right now

Rick

How about that, funny how things happen huh?

Driver

I guess. I am going to go get them now Sir

Rick

I'll stay here and wait for you

(Diver gets out of the car and Rick stays in the back)

Rick

(hears the girls coming so he gets out of the limo)

Well let's see what we got here

(In walks Natasha, Kristyn, Amanda, Martha, Jessica, Julia, Martha, and Victoria in the back. As soon as they see Rick, they start to smile. Rick has a look of shock on his face, as he walks towards the girls and he sees Victoria. Victoria has her head down looking for something in her bag. Amanda turns around and taps her)

Amanda

Vicky

Victoria

What Amanda

Amanda

Look up

(Victoria looks up and sees Rick. They make eye contact. A smile comes to the face of Victoria, she drops her bags and runs to Rick. Rick open his arms to catch Victoria who jumps into his arms and kisses him.)

Kristyn

What the hell is going on? Who is that?

Amanda

All I can say is that it's really a small world damnit

Martha

That's airport guy Kristyn

Kristyn

No fucking way, are you serious?

Jessica

Awe isn't this the sweetest moment you've ever seen before

Julia

Damn sometimes destiny works it's magic in the craziest ways

(Rick gently puts Victoria down and they stop kissing)

Victoria

What are you doing here?

Rick

I was going to ask you the same question

Victoria

I'm here for my cousin Christina wedding

Rick

(laughs)

You're fucking with me right now

Victoria

Nope, why what's so funny

Rick

While, I'm here to pick you up. Your cousin is marrying my best
friend

Victoria

Kyle, Kyle is your friend

Amanda

No fucking way

Rick

Shit Christina is your cousin

Natasha

(walks up to Rick and Victoria)

So who do we have here Vicky?

Victoria

Tash, this is Rick, the guy I told you about

Natasha

This is airport boy, wow

(Rick Laughs)

Victoria

(looks at Rick)

What?

Rick

Nothing, I mean I've had a lot of nicknames in my life but
Airport boy is just a little different

Victoria

What else was I suppose to call you, you know how many
people in the world is called Rick

Rick

(pauses and smiles)

I don't know I'm just amazed right now to see you again Vicky

Victoria

(grabs Rick's hand and holds it)

Well I told you that I'll look for you

Amanda

(walks up)

Ok, love birds can we go its hot as hell out here plus I'm hungry.
I have to say that it's nice to see you again cute boy

Rick

(smiles)

I thought they served food on the flight

Amanda

Oh no, the food looked incredible. I have to admit you guys
sure know how to treat a lady but I'm a vegetarian sweetheart

Rick

Oh damn, when I ordered the flights I didn't even think about
that. I'm sorry, we can pick up something on our way. Let's Go
then Ladies

(The ladies get into the car, then Victoria and Rick)

INT Limo

Julia

Rick from what I heard about you, you lived in New York and
worked on Wall Street. What brought you to LA? Did you burn
out or something?

Rick

Honestly, I was burnt out. But after meeting Victoria over here, I knew I wanted more in life. So when Kyle called, I didn't even hesitate to pack up and move out here

Amanda

So meeting Victoria changed your life. That's so sweet

Victoria

Shut up Amanda

Julia

Why this sounds like one of those love story fairly tales you're always reading Victoria but it's you living it

Martha

Let's see how it ends. Right Rick?

Rick

If it's up to me, then I'm going to give it my all

Jessica

So Rick you're a movie producer right?

Rick

Yeah why?

Victoria

Jessica stop, not now

Jessica

Why, this is what he does and since this seems to be your new
boyfriend why not

Victoria

(puts her head down)

Fine Jessie

Rick

What's the problem?

Victoria

nothing

Jessica

Well Vicky and I wrote a love story that we know will make a
great movie

Rick

Oh ok

Jessica

So will you read it

Victoria

You don't have too Rick

Julia

Oh yes he does

Amanda

If he really cares for you he will

Rick

Wow, is it my turn to talk or am I suppose to sit here

(The ladies are shocked and they all look at Rick)

Ok then, yes I would love to read your story, send it to me and I will check it out as soon as I get it

Jessica

What's your email, I'll send it to you right now

Rick

Rick@uniqueandcreativestudio.com

Jessica

(takes out her blackberry and starts to type on it)

I'm sending it to you from my Skydrive account

Rick

Ok

(the girls all look at Victoria and smile at her)

Kristyn

Wow looks like you found a winner Vicky

Victoria

You too Kristyn

Kristyn

What, I'm just voicing my opinion

Rick

It's fine ladies

Martha

Are you some sort of ladies man?

Rick

What you mean?

Martha

You know what I mean, are you some sort of pimp or playboy.
I've heard a lot about you Hollywood types

Victoria

How about that food, are we close

Rick

I know the best place. Trust me

(pushes the intercom button)

Driver

Yes Sir

Rick

Ok stop calling me Sir for one

Driver

Ok what do you want me to call you

Rick

Call me Rick and bring us to Escargot

Driver

Ok Rick

Martha

It's not over Rick you're going to answer all my questions soon

Rick

I'm an open book. I have nothing to hide

Martha

We'll just have to see about that

Driver

We're here

Rick

Great

Driver

Don't you need to have reservation to eat here?

Rick

What's your name my man

Driver

Tony

Rick

Well Tony you'll soon see that I don't need any of that in this town

Tony(Driver)

Wow

Rick

I'll have them bring you out a menu

(Rick gets out of the car)

Come on ladies I'm starving

(everyone gets out of the limo)

Host

Your usual spot Rick?

Rick

Yup plus, I need someone to take a menu out to my driver Tony and put whatever he orders on my tab

Host

No problem Rick

Victoria

Looks like things have changed a lot for you Mr.

Rick

What do you mean?

Victoria

We'll talk later

INT Escargot

(In walks Kyle, Christina, Anthony, Rachael, Rich, and Stephanie, they walk to the booth that Rick's at with the ladies)

Martha

CHRISTINA

(all the ladies turn around to see Christina and everyone else. Amanda gives Christina a hug. Kyle sits next to Rick and Victoria)

Amanda

Wow you look great Christina looks like the LA is treating you well

Martha

Or is it your fiancé

Jessica

There you go again Martha

Christina

I'm not going to let her get to me girl. So Girls oh how I've missed you. Did Rick take care of you

(Everyone laughs)

What what's so funny?

Amanda

Rick's, Vicky's airport guy

Christina

(look of awe on her face)

No fucking way. This is a small world. Hun didn't I tell you that Vicky and Rick would be perfect for each other

Kyle

You did sweetheart

Christina

Who would have guess that you two were some star crossed lovers

Martha

All that after a conversation at a busy airport and a kiss

Jessica

Sometimes that's all you need

Anthony

No way, this is the famous Airport girl

Rich

Wow I see why you were so obsesses with her

Rick

I was not obsessed

Rich

Oh yes you were

Ant

Ok let's not get into it

Kyle

HA, this is hilarious. Obsessed this guy was borderline stalker.
Did he tell you how he tired too...

Rick

Hey, guys ok can we keep that within the boys for now

Vicky

No I want to hear this

Rick

Oh it's nothing don't listen to them. These guys are jokers

Kyle

No let me tell y..

(Christina elbows him)

(coughs)

Ok I'm going to shut up. So ladies how was the flight?

Amanda

Well you sure know how to treat a lady that's all I can say

Martha

So Rick, are you a retired playboy like Kyle and your friend over there Anthony or do you still have your card?

Vicky

Marsha not now

Martha

Hey I have to make sure my friend doesn't get played. You know how you American Hollywood guys are

Rick

I have no clue what you are talking about

(A group of hot girls walk by and they all wave at Rick)

Girls

HI RICK

Rick

Hello ladies

(Marsha just looks at Vicky)

(Another group of girls walk by and Jennifer is with them)

Girl 1

Hey Rick

Jennifer

Hi Rick that night was great. Call us whenever you want to do it
again

(Walks away)

Martha

Retired shit looks like your still knee deep in the life Mr.
Hollywood

(Rick just shakes his head and looks down)

Vicky

Don't you have anything to say?

Rich

Come on pimp say something

Martha

Even his friend called him a pimp. Vicky don't do it. Leave this
one alone. He's no Mr. Right, He's Mr. Wrong

Rick

(looks at Vicky)

I'm not that guy you think I am trust me. I won't lie I've lived a crazy life but don't judge me

Amanda

That's not what Christina told us about you

(Rick looks at Christina)

Christina

I'm sorry Rick. It was before I got to know you. Kyle told me that. I mean Rick the ladies do love you

Rick

Damn, Kyle

Kyle

Sorry bro, I didn't know but it's the truth bro

Rick

So this is what you guys tell people about me

Rich

I mean bro it's the truth

Rick

Damn just throw me under the bus why don't you

Anthony

Hold up, I'm not going to allow y'all to gang up on my boy.
Deep down Rick's a great guy and a gem for anyone to be with.
Isn't that right sweetheart

Rachael

You know I thought Rick was a pimp, playboy, ladies man, and
everything under that category until..

(holds Anthony's hand)

I was going through a rough time and Rick came out of nowhere
like a knight in shining armor and help me make the right
decision. He's a great guy. He truly is

Martha

That's so sweet but he's still a player and not the type of guy for
me friend

Victoria

(Looks at Rick)

Damn looks like this town changed you. I thought it was destiny
that brought us back together but it was just the devil playing a
cruel joke or maybe it's telling me to go back to what I know

Rick

Hold up. Its not like that, please trust me

(his phone rings, it's the club)

Hello...Wait what. What do you mean Jose hurt. What happen?
Fire, I'm on my way.

(Looks at Vicky)

I have to go can we talk about this later?

Vicky

Nothing to talk about Rick. Good bye, go take care of your
emergency

(Rick takes a deep breathe)

Kyle

What happen to the club?

Rick

Nothing, I can't handle. Don't worry about it stay here. I don't
belong here anyways let me get back to business

(Rick gets up and walks away)

Rachael

Y'all underestimate that guy. He's a great guy

Martha

Yeah if you want to deal with a player. Once a player always a
player

Kyle

(Looks at Christina)

Let me go and check out the club. I should be there

Christina

I'm coming with you.

Anthony'

Let's all go

EXT Club

Smoke coming out of the windows and doors of the club. You
see Jose being put into an ambulance and it drives away.   Rick
is sitting on the sidewalk outside of the club talking to the cops.
Kyle and the group rolls up. Kyle walks over to Rick and puts his
hand on his shoulder)

Kyle

It's going to be alright, the place is insured

Rick

It's not ok, it will never be ok ever again

(gets up)

I've lost it all tonight. I'm going to the hospital to check on Jose.
They don't know if he is going to make it.

Kyle

I'll come with you

Rick

Please don't. I'm done I give up. It's time for a change

Kyle

What do you mean?

Rick

I mean I'm thinking about leaving. You guys don't need me around anymore. You don't need the lone wolf in this crew. So this is probably good bye Kyle

(Rick walks away)

Kyle

Rick Wait

Martha

Let him go

Kyle

(turns to Marsha)

Listen, I don't know you but I do know him and he may have some flaws but no one here is perfect. That man is the best man I know and I won't lose him not now. He's the glue that keeps everything together. So please leave me alone unless you're trying to help in a positive way

Christina

(walks up and holds Kyle hand)

Go be with him, he might not show it but he needs you tonight. The girls and I will take the limo home

(Rich and Anthony walk up)

Rich

I think we went too far at the dinner table. I didn't think it
would affect him like that

Anthony

He does everything and anything for us but we never ask him
what we can do for him. We didn't even see that he was
hurting on the inside

Rich

Ever since that girl called him Hollywood, he's been down and
tonight didn't help

Kyle

What kind of friends are we

Ant

I don't know but we have to fix this ASAP

Rich and Kyle

Agreed

Ant

I have a plan

(Rick to Himself)

After that night I knew love wasn't for me but everywhere I
went all I could see was love. I wanted to be alone so I went
down to the Santa Monica Pier and it was there.

(Cut to: Santa Monica Pier and you see couples holding hands, sharing ice cream. Kids playing with each other while their parents watch)

I just couldn't escape it. I even went to Runyon Canyon to exercise and damnit it was couples day there too. Then I decided to walk Hollywood Blvd to check out the weirdos and it seem like it was weirdo couple day there too. So after two days of that God playing a cruel joke on me "I decided to just stay at home and chill. The club was about to be renovated. Our show was on hiatus until the fall and the wedding was happening in a month and the ladies didn't want me around. So now I'm here looking up at my ceiling listen to Bob Marley.

INT Rick's Loft 2 days later

(Rick is laying on his bed looking up at the ceiling. His phone is ringing and he doesn't move. Then there's knocking at the front door)

                    Ant

Open the door bro I know you're in there I see your car and I hear the radio. I'm not going to leave. I will stay here and knock your door until it falls apart

(Rick finally gets up. He has his boxers, t shirt, flip fops, and robe on. He opens the door. Ant and Rachael walks in and goes to sit in the living room)

                    Rick

            What do you want?

Ant

Damn man it smells in here

Rick

What do you want?

Ant

What's up man talk to me

Rick

If this is some sort in intervention, you both can leave right now.
I don't want it Once the club is rebuilt, I'm leaving. I'm thinking
about moving to Toronto or even Russia and starting over. At
least no one knows me over there. This town ruin me

Rachael

You know you came to my aid in a similar situation

Rick

So

Rachael

So I know what you are feeling right now

Rick

Yeah but look at you, things worked out for you and it didn't for
me

Rachael

How do you know? Did you even try?

Rick

She won't return my phone calls or text messages. Plus her girls won't let me see her. It's fine, I'll be airight. I don't want you two to worry about little old me. I'll survive

Ant

Listen to me my man, and answer this question

Rick

What

Ant

Is she the one?

Rick

You already know the answer to that question

Ant

I want to hear it from you. So is she?

Rick

Yes

Ant

Are you ready to anything to get her

Rick

Yes

Ant

Perfect. I'm working on a plan to have you too to have some private time but you're going to have to bring it when you do see her again. Are you ready for that?

Rick

Yeah I think so

Ant

Don't think just do it

(Ant and Rachael gets and up)

The next time I call you answer the call Sir

Rick

Why, why are you helping me so much? Why did you come here?

Ant

(looks at Rachael)

You know you did something for me that no one has ever done before. You helped me find love

(holds onto Rachael's hand tighter)

And you did it just to do it unselfishly and that means a lot for me. I will forever be in your debt. Just look at this as a way of starting to pay you back

Rick

You don't owe me anything

Ant

(while walking out of the loft)

I'm old school my friend. Just answer the call

INT Coffee Bean

(it's packed and Rick is sitting at a table looking out of the window. An old couple walks up to Rick's table)

Old Man

Do you mind if we sit here

Rick

(turns to look at the couple)

Oh no I don't mind please sit

Old Man

Thank you young man

Old Lady

What's the matter son? is it love?

Old Man

Angie please leave the young man alone. Can't you see, he has a lot on his mind

Angie

I can, Chris, the poor boy has something eating him up on the inside

Rick

It's fine, I'm okay really

Angie

Are you going to lie to an old lady

Rick

(grins)

Ok fine, but I don't think you two would understand

Chris

Try us

Rick

Ok well I met the girl of my dreams but she saw a piece of my past life and it destroyed everything. But what she doesn't know is that, I would give it all up for her

Angie

(laughs and holds Chris's hand)

Ah Chris brings back memories

Chris

Son in my heyday, I was the head of the biggest studio in this town. I had the reputation of being the worst ladies man and I mean I was, I was bad. Then one day, I saw an Angel, and I knew at that moment she was the one for me. She was the game changer, the one I would leave it all for but she knew my reputation and she wouldn't have anything to do with me at all. I had to pull all the stops to even get a coffee with her. Once she did, I made sure she knew exactly what I was thinking and how much she meant to me. My advice to you is, if she's the one, don't let anything stop you. Nothing at all because you don't want to get to my age and still be here looking outside of the window wondering what if. You only live once right. Make sure you live it to the fullest

(They get up and the old man pats Rick on his shoulder)

Good Luck son

Angie

Next time we see each other, I hope you look better on the inside

(They leave)

(Rick Continues to look out of the window and then his phone rings)

Hello

Rachael

She's at my house alone. Good luck sweetheart, I have faith in you. Bye

Rick

(Rick looks out of the window and sees Angie and Chris holding hands while crossing the street. He then looks at his phone and car keys on the table. A model type girl stops at the table)

Model

Is anyone sitting here

Rick

No

Girl

So are you single because you are really cute

Rick

You know what? you are an extremely beautiful woman. If this was the old me, I would get to know you better, wine and dine you, and pull out all the stops to sleep with you. But there is something I must go and do. So all I am going to say is have a wonderful day and I hope you find true love one day

(Rick gets up and grabs his stuff and proceeds to run out of the door to his car)

EXT Rachael house

(Rick pulls up hops out of the car and runs to the door and starts to knock harshly)

INT House

(Vicky hears the knocks and walks down the stairs to the door)

Vicky

Who is it?

EXT House

Rick

'It's me Vicky, Rick. Can we Talk?

INT House

Vicky

There's nothing for us to talk about Rick. I see what you are, you're Mr. Hollywood. Why don't you go live at the playboy Mansion? You and Hugh would probably be great friends

EXT House

Rick

Listen you have the wrong image of me

INT House

Vicky

So if I asked you a question will you tell me the truth?

EXT House

>Rick

>I always do

INT House

>Vicky

>Are you a playboy?

EXT House

>Rick

>That's not fair

INT House

>Vicky

>Life isn't fair sometimes. Answer the question

>Rich

No I mean I mean maybe I am but all that happen after I thought I would never see you again. I really wasn't one when we first met

INT House

>Vicky

>What do you mean?

EXT House

Rick

Can you open the door, I want to see you while I'm talking to you

INT House

Vicky

Maybe we're not suppose to get what we want

EXT House

Rick

It doesn't have to be that way Vicky, Please Vicky, just open the door

Vicky

Fine

(opens the door and just looks at Rick in his eyes. Rick glances down and sees her bags all packed)

This is what I was afraid of

(Rick pauses and just looks at Vicky)

Vicky

What is it Rick, why are you here?

Rick

I needed to see you and talk to you. I needed to know

Vicky

Who told you I was here

Rick

A friend

Vicky

I know something was fishy, I told her I needed a place to think
but it's too late Rick I'm leaving and heading home. I have
someone waiting for me that I know will never cheat on me

Rick

What? No Vicky, please give me a chance

Vicky

I can't Rick, I can't be hurt again

Rick

But I won't I couldn't hurt you please don't go

Vicky

I have too, my plane leaves in a few hours I have a cab coming

Rick

What about Christina's wedding

Vicky

She'll understand, she knows what I've been through before
and why I'm leaving

Rick

Can I ask you a question?

Vicky

what did you need to know

Rick

(Takes a deep breathe)

I needed to tell you how I feel about you Vicky. I needed you to remember that day we met at the Airport. I needed you to remember that guy because he's still here right in front of you. Don't believe the lies, just look at me in my eyes, don't be scared, I am still that guy that you fell in love with and believe me I fell too and I still haven't stopped falling. That day changed me and made me realize I wanted more in life, and it made me go after it. One day I will tell you all the ways I tried to find you but that's beside the point. These past few years I was pretending to be something, I'm not because it was the only way I knew to try to patch the hole in my heart that you showed me that day was there. I knew that moment I met you that you were the one and destiny brought us back together. So please Vicky give love a chance, give me a chance and let me show you the real me

Vicky

What about all those ladies you have? How do I know I'm not some notch on your wall

Rick

(moves closer to Vicky)

They never meant anything but you do, you mean everything to me. They were like gravel that's used to patch a pothole. It never really does the job

Vicky

What

Rick

(takes Vicky by the hands)

I learned something from this old couple today. I learned that you have to give your all for love if you really want it so here I am at my most vulnerable moment telling you, that when you know you just know and I knew from our first time meeting that you were the one, that will fill the hole inside of me and I am the one that will do the same for you

Vicky

(Release her hands from Rick)

How do you Kn..

(Rick grabs Vicky hand, turns her around ,and kisses her passionately. Vicky kisses him back. They separate and stare at each other)

Rick

That is how you know

Vicky

(starts to cry)

No I can't, I have to go

Rick

Why

Vicky

Because I have someone waiting for me back home

Rick

Your tears say it all, you don't love him like you love me and you know that

Vicky

You might be right but he's the safer choice

Rick

There's no safety in love, it's a dangerous game but when it's real it's worth everything

Vicky

I'm sorry Rick, I just can't risk it

(Vicky's cab pulls up and the driver honks the horn)

My ride to the Airport is here. I have to go Rick

Rick

Then I'll take you

Vicky

No my cab is here, you don't have too

Rick

Yes I do

Vicky

Fine

(Rick goes over to the cab driver and gives him a hundred and he leaves)

Rick

Ok let's go

(Rick grabs Vicky's bags and they get into Rick's car)

EXT Outside of the Airport)

(Rick gets out and opens the door for Vicky. He then goes to the trunk and gets her bags)

Rick

Well here we are

Vicky

(wipes her eyes and looks at Rick)

Rick

So is this the end

Vicky

Yes it is, I mean It might be, I just don't know anymore Rick. All I know is that I have to leave here it hurts too much to stay

Rick

It's the perfect place to end it at the beginning

Vicky

The beginning

Rick

Yeah we first met at a airport and now

Vicky

Don't say it, it's just going to make matters worse, bye Rick

(Vicky gives Rick a kiss on the check, turns around and walks away)

Rick

(stands there and watches her enter the terminal)

Airport Security

Sir you have to move your car now

Rick

(looks at the officer)

Huh oh sorry officer, I'll move it now

(Rick gets into his car and starts the engine, he sits there for a second)

Security

Move the car now

Rick

(looks at the officer and then looks up to the sky. He quickly jumps out of the car and heads towards the terminal)

Officer

I will have your car towed

Rick

If that's the cost I have to pay for love then I'll gladly pay it

INT Airport

(Rick sees Vicky walking towards security to get into her terminal)

Rick

Vicky, Vicky, Vicky wait please wait

(Vicky turns around and sees Rick running toward her)

Vicky

Rick, what are you doing?

Rick

Everything I have to do

Vicky

What do you mean?

Rick

Tell me you love him more than me and I will leave you alone but if you don't then I'm getting on the plane with you right now, I'm not going to let you go not now

Vicky

Rick

Rick

Tell me you love him more

Vicky

I... Do..

(Rick kisses Vicky passionately and she kisses him back. Everyone around applauds them. An old lady walks up to her)

Old Lady

Trust me when I tell you this, go for it

Vicky

(wipes her tears and looks at the old lady)

Thank you

Rick

(puts his hand out for Vicky)

Vicky

(looks at his hand and then looks at Rick in his eyes)

My mother always told me that the eyes don't lie

Rick

So what's it going to be? What are my eyes telling you? Are you going to give love a chance

Vicky

Yes Rick

(she grabs Rick hand)

So where do we go from here

Rick

The moon

Vicky

Are you sure you only want to be with one woman. I mean you have them all now

Rick

They were all just practice, so when the right one came around I would know

Vicky

So I guess you really like me, huh

Rick

Absolutely, so are we getting on this plane or going back to the house

Vicky

(smiles)

Back to the house

Rick

Ooo, cuz I sure didn't have a ticket for this plane

Vicky

You're an fool

Rick

A fool in love

EXT Airport

(They walk out of the Airport to see a tow truck pulling up to tow Rick's car)

Rick

(running to his car)

Hold up, I'm here

Officer

I didn't want to but my boss told me too, you're a lucky guy

(the officer signals the tow truck to leave)

Did you find love?

Rick

(Holding Vicky hands)

Yes I did

Officer

Great now get out of here before I really tow your car

Vicky

Thank you officer

(Rick and Vicky get into the car and they drive off)

EXT Rachael house

(Rick and Vicky pull up to the house and walk into it)

INT House

(The front door opens up and in walks Rick and Vicky)

Martha

What are you two doing, oh no Vicky don't tell me you did

Amanda

Shut up Martha and let the girl make her own decisions

Jessica

Yea, these two were destine to be together

Rich

(walks up to Rick)

I'm sorry.

Rick

Don't be

Rich

No you're my best friend

Kyle

He's all our best friend and I am sorry too bro

Ant

Group hug

(Ant grabs Rich, Kyle, and Rick and they all hug. Rick doesn't let go of Vicky hand)

Kristyn

Oh my God do you see that

Natasha

What it's ok for men to hug

Kristyn

Oh no not that he never let go of Vicky hand, oh this is serious.
They're going to be next ladies

Rick

There you have it, my story on how my true love happen.

Cut To; Montage of the wedding

Rick

So Kyle and Christina wedding was beautiful. I was the best
man and Vicky was the Maid of Honor. I tried to convince Vicky
that we should just move to Canada but she wanted to stay in
LA we even became business partners. We co-produced the
movie that she co-wrote with Jessica

Cut to Montage of the movie being filmed

Rick

And it was a hit. We did everything together and not just us the
whole crew Anthony, Rachael, Kyle and Christina, Rich and
Stephanie, and even Amanda, Jessica, and Kristyn moved out
here. We were one big family and it was great. You know, I
didn't know what I was missing until I found love.

Cut To Vicky and Rick walking down the street holding hands
and you see that's she's pregnant

Rick

I even left the club life alone. Jose healed up and I promoted
him to club manager. He has the club packed every night with

no problems. I hardly have to be there now. You know what, I did run into that old couple again, matter of fact Chris helped me get my new job, Head of Sony Pictures. He really was connected. This is to show you, that you never know who you are going to meet and how they can impact your life if you just take time out and talk to them, this lead me to the love of my life and my dream job, So take a chance and see where it can lead you.

Cut To: Rick getting out of a limo, walking the red carpet, and waving to the people taking pictures with Victoria by his side.

Rick

While bye for now, I have a premier to go too. I hope one day you too will find love

The End

www.ingramcontent.com/pod-product-compliance
Lightning Source LLC
Chambersburg PA
CBHW060748180626
46818CB00002B/499